D0624320

Leopold the Lion

Written by Denise Brennan-Nelson

Illustrated by Ruth McNally Barshaw

Jack and Ella were playing in the backyard when they heard a rustle and deep purr coming from the bushes.

Shoving branches aside they stared right into the eyes of . . .

...A LION?!

"What a pretty lion!" said Ella. Lion sniffed Ella and then licked her with his long tongue.

Ella giggled. Lion's amber eyes twinkled and with a graceful leap, he landed on the trampoline. Jack and Ella watched as Lion performed somersaults, twists, and backflips.

When the sun dipped behind the oak tree, Ella whispered to Jack, "Can we keep him?"

It wasn't hard to get past Mom.

And it wasn't hard to get past Dad.

They were halfway up the stairs when Grandpa muttered, "Doesn't look like an indoor cat to me."

Jack and Ella knew what they were supposed to do.
They fed him. Made sure he had plenty to drink.
Played with him. And gave him a bath.

Lion had a ferocious appetite! Jack and Ella were always rummaging through the cupboards and the refrigerator in search of food.

It wasn't hard to get past Mom.

And it wasn't hard to get past Dad.

But Grandpa always had something to say.

"Cats like meat, not munchies."

Fall arrived with a new schedule.

Every day, before Jack and Ella left for school,
they made sure Lion had enough to eat and drink.
And Lion stayed busy while they were away.

Jack and Ella hurried home after school every day, eager to play with Lion.

At first, Lion would run to greet them, playfully knocking them down and showering them with big, wet lion licks.

After a while, Lion stopped greeting them.

Ella missed Lion's kisses.

One afternoon, when they returned from school, Grandpa handed them a piece of paper. "Found this in the mailbox today," he said.

When they got to their room they read it.

LOST LION:
Name: Leopold, loves trampolines.
If found return to the circus.

Ella crouched down next to Lion. She stared at the picture, and then at Lion.

"Leopold?"

When Lion lifted his head Ella noticed his fur was knotted and tangled and the sparkle in his amber eyes was missing.

The next morning, Jack and Ella prepared to take Lion back to the circus.

It wasn't hard to get past Mom.

It wasn't hard to get past Dad.

But Grandpa ...

Grandpa was standing at the door. "Need a ride?"

When they arrived at the circus, Jack and Ella had to pull and tug to get Lion out of the car.

"Excuse me," Jack announced when they got inside. "We're here to return Leopold."

The circus employees laughed.

"That isn't Leopold," the trainer said. And to prove his point he gave Leopold the signal to do a somersault. Leopold didn't budge.

He held up a hoop and blew his whistle. Leopold just lay there.

"This lion is no performer," the trainer said.

The other circus animals stared at Leopold.
Leopold kept his head down.

"Yes, he is!" Ella cried. But she had to agree
that Leopold didn't look like a performer.

It was a quiet car ride home with Leopold.

Finally, Grandpa spoke. "I think you know what you have to do."

Jack and Ella looked at Leopold and nodded.

They fed him lots of healthy food.
Made sure he had plenty of water to drink.
And every day, they took him outside to play.

At first, Leopold didn't want to go but Ella
and Jack insisted.

And when Jack and Ella were at school Grandpa
made sure Leopold didn't lie around all day.
They had other things to do.

Before long, Leopold's mane was shiny.

He held his head up proudly.

And, once again, his amber eyes sparkled.

Especially when he was performing for everyone ...

... at Jack and Ella's backyard circus.

For Rach Bach and Al Pal
– Love, Momma Chomma

*

To my cubs, Lisa and Matt, Joe and Cait,
Katie, and Emily, and their little cubs.

– Ruth McNally Barshaw

Sleeping Bear Press®
2395 South Huron Parkway, Suite 200
Ann Arbor, MI 48104
www.sleepingbearpress.com

Printed and bound in the United States.

10 9 8 7 6 5 4 3 2 1

Library of Congress Cataloging-in-Publication Data

Brennan-Nelson, Denise.
Leopold the Lion / by Denise Brennan-Nelson ; illustrated by Ruth McNally Barshaw.
pages cm
Summary: Jack and Ella are thrilled to take a friendly lion
as their pet, but when Leopold the Lion grows chubby and despondent,
they must seek a way to make him healthy again.
ISBN 978-1-58536-828-0
1. Lions as pets—Fiction. 2. Food habits—Fiction. 3. Brothers and sisters—Fiction.]
I. Barshaw, Ruth McNally, illustrator. II. Title.
PZ7.B75165Leo 2015
[E]—dc23   2015001570